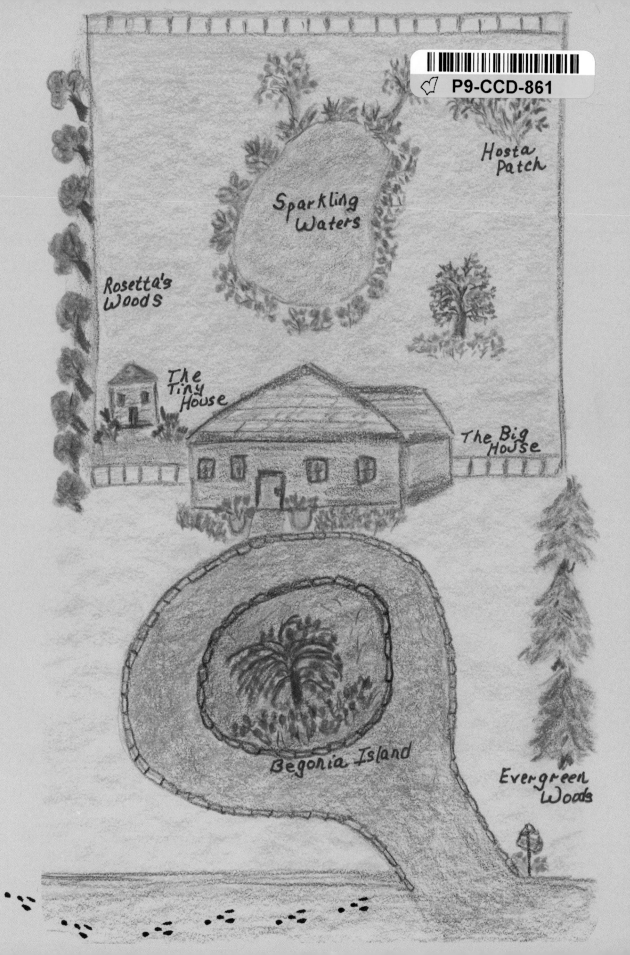

The Flowerpot Bunny Mom

Written by Dr. Carolyn Rehm

Illustrated by Agnes Schanck and Emily Rehm

Library of Congress Cataloging-in-Publication Data
Rehm, Carolyn, 1952-
Rosetta, The Flowerpot Bunny Mom/by Carolyn Rehm

Summary: A fictional account of the celebration of the
Flowerpot Bunny Mom's Birthday and the adventures it brings
1. Bunnies-fiction.

ISBN 978-0-9755390-3-3

Cover and layout designed by Rosemary Carroll and Patti Bishop
All artwork by Agnes Schanck and Emily Rehm
All photography by Carolyn Rehm
Printed in China
Published by Fith Avenue Press
413 Salt Pond Road, Bethany Beach, DE 19930
A portion of the proceeds
from the sale of this book will be donated
by the author to help children with special needs.

I would like to dedicate this book
to my Mom, Agnes Schanck,
whose life was an inspiration to me
and my entire family.

Her charming illustrations will
delight many readers for years to come!

She will be dearly missed.
1925–2008

The sun was beginning to set on the western horizon. Brilliant reds, oranges, and yellows exploded in the shimmering sky, creating a bright palette of colors. The summer trees were vibrant green and swayed to the tune of a gentle breeze. Mother robins chirped as they flew to their nests, and bumblebees buzzed around fragrant tiger lilies. Hummingbirds fluttered as they drank nectar from flowers, and fireflies flickered. It was a perfect July evening.

In this peaceful neighborhood, a solitary brown rabbit sat on the blanket of grass and watched the day end and twilight softly emerge. Her ears were ever listening, her eyes were ever watchful. Amidst all this beauty, she sighed with contentment.

This was the rabbit's world; the place she had called home from the day she was born. Today she was five years old. She was very excited because her family had planned a big birthday party tonight to celebrate!

Distracted from her pleasant thoughts, the rabbit spotted a lady leaving the house nearby. Watering can in hand, the lady began to sprinkle the flowers that filled the pots around her deck. Spotting the rabbit, she waved and said hello. The bunny mom turned to accept this greeting, as she had many times before. She had no fear of this human, and, in fact, enjoyed sharing this place with the lady and her family. The bunny mom smiled as she thought of the many memories they had made together.

"How are you and your little ones doing?" the lady asked the rabbit. "I see them running all over the yard, playing and munching on flowers. Are there any new nests I should know about?" She laughed and called out goodnight as she went back into the house.

Just then the rabbit was joined by Poppy, her lifelong mate, who hopped out from the woods behind her.

"Hello, my darling Rosetta," Poppy greeted her. "Isn't it a beautiful sunset?"

"Why yes, it is!" Rosetta replied. "I was thinking about tonight and I am so excited. It's been such a long time since we've all been together."

"You're right," Poppy said as he sat down close beside her. "All of our children and grandchildren from the Hosta Patch, Sparkling Waters, and Begonia Island will soon be here. Daisy's family from the Evergreen Woods is already waiting for you."

"That's wonderful! Let's go see them!" Rosetta exclaimed, as she and Poppy headed off into the woods behind the tiny house.

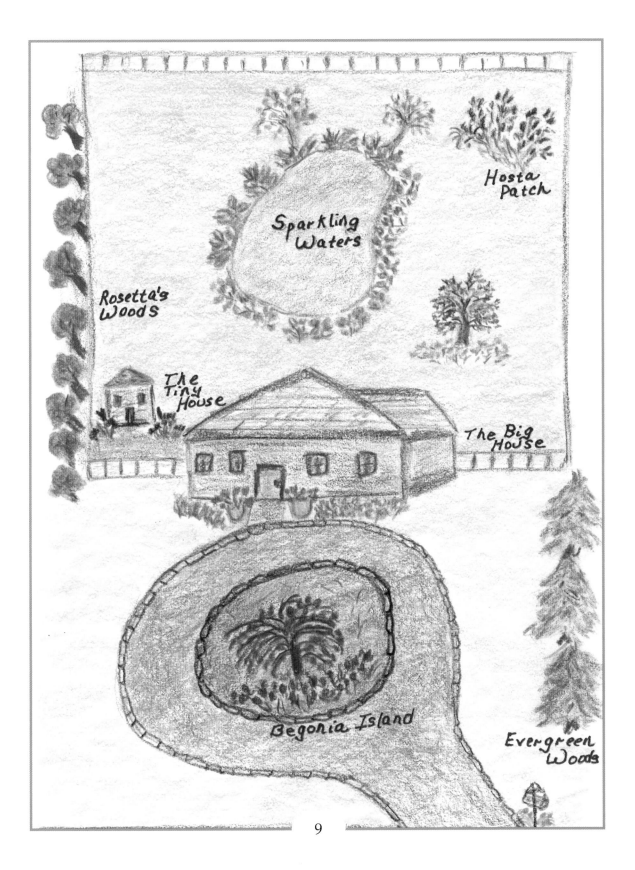

Amidst the thicket and underbrush in these woods, the rabbits had created a warren, or maze of tunnels, in which they lived. There were also shallow holes, or forms, that were wider and could fit many rabbits together. Nearby there was tasty grass and clover to dine on. The borders were lined with delicious flowers of all kinds. It was truly a bunny paradise!

Daisy sat in one of the larger forms and saw her mother approaching.

"There she is!" Daisy announced to her family.

"It's Grandma Rosie!" the five grandchildren chimed in together. "Happy birthday, happy birthday!"

Rosetta gathered them close to her for a big hug and kissed their little noses.

"Oh my wonderful grandchildren," Rosetta said. "How it does my heart good to see you. And what beautiful flower necklaces you're wearing!"

"Mama made them for us to celebrate your birthday," Holly, Daisy's youngest, explained. "There is one for you too. We also made dandelion soup and forget-me-not cake for all of us!"

"Well, that is just delightful. I am very hungry!" Rosetta exclaimed.

"Come, Mother," Daisy said as she led her to a soft spot in the center of the hole. "Sit here while we wait for the rest of the family. What have you been doing today?"

"I was just over by the house," Rosetta said as she made herself comfortable.

"Did you see the lady?" Daisy asked.

"Yes, I did. She was busy watering her flowers."

"Wouldn't she be surprised if she knew about the big party tonight?" Daisy asked, handing her mom the necklace of pink roses.

"I'm sure she would be. It's a shame we can't invite her to join us," Rosetta said as she put on the necklace.

One of Daisy's babies, named Timmy, who had big black eyes and a quick mind, asked, "Invite a human to our party? That certainly wouldn't be safe, would it?"

Rosetta laughed. "You don't know this particular human mom, Timmy. She would never hurt us."

"Do you think she would like forget-me-not cake?" Holly asked.

"I'm sure she would love it!" Rosetta replied.

Timmy was not convinced. "I just don't trust humans and I think they should stay with their own families!" he said with a thump of his foot.

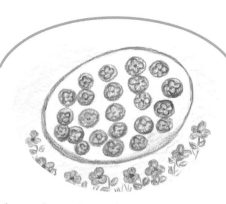

It was just then that the other bunny families began to arrive. Rose, Jack, and their three children, Lavender, Grace, and Nutmeg, came from the Sparkling Waters. They wore hats made of bluebells and hugged their grandparents tightly. Marigold and Dandelion came with their families from the Hosta Patch and Begonia Island. Everyone was very excited as the form quickly filled with rabbits, young and old, huddling together on that warm summer evening.

"Now where is Cracker Jack?" Poppy asked.

"He's probably busy checking out the area around the woods," Marigold responded proudly. "You know him – always trying to protect us. He wouldn't want some cat or fox to ruin our party."

"You know your brother," Rosetta explained. "He doesn't want a repeat of what happened to me four years ago."

"What was that, Grandma?" one of Dandelion's little ones, named Amanda, asked. She was busy munching on the begonia cookies her mom had made for the party.

"Well, that is an interesting, but scary story," Rosetta replied. As all the bunnies quieted down to listen, she began to tell the tale.

"When I was younger," she began, "I was very bold and creative when choosing a spot for each of my nests."

"Grandma was a little silly with her nest-building, if you ask me!" Poppy exclaimed.

"I guess I was," Rosetta agreed. "On this particular occasion, I was planning a nest by the edge of the Sparkling Waters when all of a sudden I saw a big red fox very close by."

"Eeeeek!" the grandchildren screamed. "Did you get away?"

"Yes, I did escape. I started to hop at top speed but, in my hurry, I didn't see an old fence post in the dark forest. There were wires attached to it and I caught my ear on one of them. The pain was very bad, but I couldn't stop until I was back in the form with your grandpa."

"Yes," said Poppy, "I nursed her back to health but her ear was never the same. That's why her left ear is split down the middle," he explained as he pointed to Rosetta's ear.

"Does your ear hurt?" Lavender asked with concern.

"No, my little one," Rosetta said. "Not anymore – but it's a reminder to always be watchful when you are making a nest. You should also be especially careful when you're running away from a big red fox!" She laughed and wiggled her split ear at them. They giggled in reply.

"Tell them where you made some of your other nests, Mom," Daisy said.

Rosetta closed her eyes as she thought for a moment. "Well," she said, "there was this beautiful flowerpot....and oh, there was the time I made a nest right in the center of the vast grasses between here and the Sparkling Waters. I thought it was safe, but a little human girl stepped into it. The lady covered the nest with a small table, which I thought was odd. But it did make it nice and shady when I had to nurse my babies!"

"What else did she do?" Nutmeg asked, as he bit into a piece of snapdragon brownie.

"She took all the babies out of the nest when the big grass-cutting machines came that made the ground rumble!" Rosetta continued.

"I don't like those noisy machines," Nutmeg said with a shudder.

"I do, I do!" Timmy exclaimed. "I like the way they make my tummy shake. The lady would not have to save me - I am very brave!"

"I'm sure you are, Timmy," Rosetta said. "That day everything turned out fine because the lady returned the babies to the nest. I, however, learned that it would be better to hide a nest under the sunflowers or among the milkweeds, than in the vast grasses."

At that moment, a very large rabbit jumped out of the bushes and into the form. "Hell-o everyone!" Cracker Jack called out.

"Welcome, welcome," the rabbits replied.

"I have just finished checking out the area around the woods and I am pleased to report that all is well," Cracker Jack told them.

"Thank you, dear," Rosetta said as they rubbed noses. "Now come sit with us and have some of these yummy treats."

"Ah, clover soup - my favorite," he said. As Cracker Jack went to sit down, he whispered to his brothers, "We need to keep an eye out for the tom cat. He's out prowling around on the other side of the grasses. I don't want to worry anyone." His brothers nodded in response and agreed to stay alert.

"Grandma, can you tell us another story, please?" Amanda asked.

"Tell us about the flowerpot nests," Grace cried. "We love that story!" She hopped up and down in anticipation.

Rosetta settled down and gazed lovingly at her family. There were so many more of her children who lived in the distant woods. All of them had a special place in her heart. She smiled as she began her story.

"As I mentioned, I once found a beautiful flowerpot up near the big house. It seemed like a perfect spot to build a nest and so I did! One day the lady and her children discovered the nest."

"Were you worried?" Holly asked.

"No, not at first," Rosetta replied. "Then one day I jumped into the nest and all my babies were gone!"

"That's terrible," Grace whispered. "What did you do?"

"I looked in the window and saw that the lady had put my babies into cages. She told me not to worry, but she was concerned that the babies would fall out of the nest and get lost or hurt. So, I spent the next three weeks close to the house and, don't you know, the lady brought the babies back out to me. They had grown a lot and were very healthy. She had fed them and cared for them and returned them safely."

"Yes, and while we were in the house, the lady's children gave us our names!" Daisy added.

"That's right," Rosetta said. "Those five babies are all here tonight – Daisy, Rose, Marigold, Dandelion, and Cracker Jack. They were all named by humans – isn't that amazing?" The grandchildren nodded in reply.

"Were you afraid in the big house?" Nutmeg asked his mom.

"Maybe at first," Rose answered. "They didn't hurt us, however, and always brought us yummy clover and flowers to eat."

"I would have attacked them!" Timmy shouted.

"I tried that," Cracker Jack said, laughing. "It did no good at all, so I watched and waited for a chance to escape. I kept a sharp eye out for trouble and tried my famous kung fu moves on the lady."

"I bet you scared her," Timmy said.

"I don't think so!" Cracker Jack replied. "She and her children never hurt us. Even their dogs were friendly."

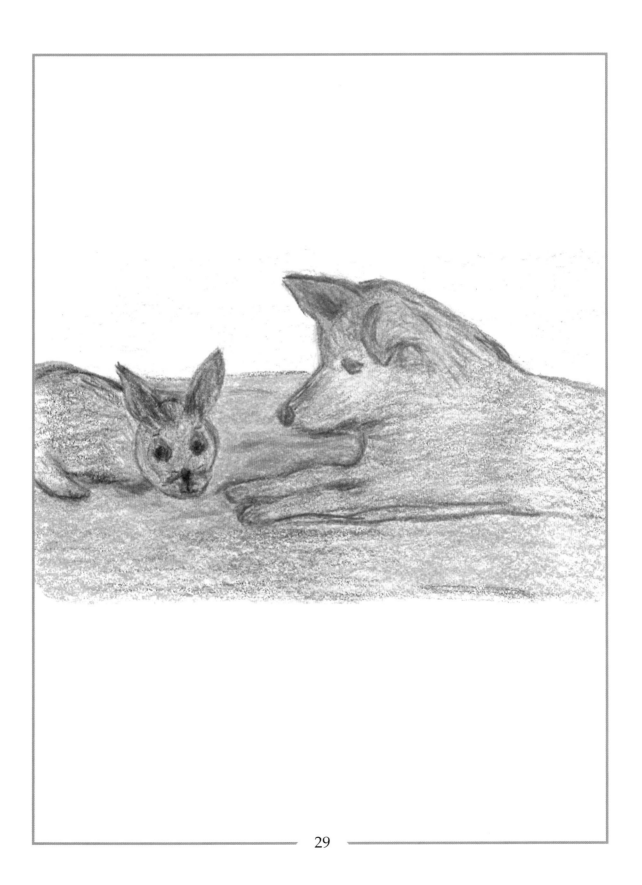

"Did you ever have any other flowerpot nests?" Lavender asked.

"Only one other time in front of the big house, and the lady took the babies for a short while. They were returned to me as well, and now live in the warren over by the pond," Rosetta explained.

"Why do you think the lady took your babies each time, Mom?" Dandelion asked. "It just doesn't seem like something a human would do."

"Well," Rosetta said, pausing to think, "I'm sure that she believed she was helping and was really worried that the babies were in danger. Or perhaps she simply loved baby bunnies," she said with a smile.

Everyone laughed, but Cracker Jack shouted, "Quiet, everyone! I hear something coming." He and his brothers hopped away from the group to investigate, when all of a sudden a large black-and-white cat jumped into the thicket. The cat grinned when he saw the rabbits.

"Ah, having a party?" he asked with a sneer. "This is my lucky day!"

"Take your babies and run!" Cracker Jack ordered as he jumped in front of the mean old cat. He put his hands up, ready for a fight.

"Everyone run to the tiny house! We can hide under it," Rosetta called as she scooted them along.

The bunnies scattered as the cat stalked closer and closer. He swiped a paw at Cracker Jack, who fell back onto the ground. At that moment, the cat spotted Timmy, who had tripped on a twig and stumbled into a hole nearby. The cat leapt toward him and went to grab him with his mouth when everyone was startled to hear, "Woof, woof. Woof, woof!"

A little black dog barked fiercely at the cat and a voice called out loudly, "Scat, you big old cat! Leave that bunny alone!" The lady stood nearby, shining a flashlight on the scene.

The cat raced away and Cracker Jack sat motionless as he watched the lady and the dog.

"Now, little one, don't be afraid," she said to Timmy. "You are safe. Go and find your family." As she spoke, the lady picked up the little dog.

Timmy looked up at the lady's face and felt no fear. He smiled at her and then hopped off to find his mother. The lady said to her dog, "Come on, Chloe, let's go back inside. I think you deserve a special treat for spotting that bunny in trouble."

Chloe licked the lady's face in agreement as they headed back to the house.

Rosetta, Poppy, and all the other rabbits ran to Timmy and took him back to the form. After a short time, everyone relaxed and started to party again. They all enjoyed the pansy pastries with mint jelly and gobbled up the geranium sandwiches washed down with lots of honeysuckle punch.

The grandchildren played games such as blossom hopscotch and berry catch. They rolled in the grass and hopped under the moonlight.

Later in the evening, Timmy snuggled up to his grandma. He whispered in her ear, "I wish we could have invited the lady to our party."

"I know, dear," Rosetta replied with a sigh. "I feel the same way."

As the stars shone brightly on that warm summer evening, the air was filled with the sounds of crickets chirping and bunnies singing "Happy Birthday."

Very early the next morning, Rosetta hopped out onto the grass to eat. She noticed that there were lots of people on the deck and by the Sparkling Waters. They were putting up balloons and decorations, setting up tables and chairs. Rosetta saw the lady and her children laughing and talking.

"They must be having a party of their own," Rosetta said to herself. "I wish I could thank the lady for last night." Just then she had a wonderful idea.

Later that day, as the lady was walking in the yard with her daughters, she saw something lying in the grass. Bending over, she picked up a fragrant chain of lovely pink roses.

"Look at this," she said. "Isn't it beautiful?"

"How do you think it got here?" Emily asked.

"I don't know," her mom replied.

"I saw the bunny mom sitting over here on the lawn earlier today," Catherine said. "Do you think she left it for you?"

The lady thought for a moment as she stared off into the woods. "That would not surprise me at all," she said with a smile. "The bunny mom would do something thoughtful like that. Let's go back to the party, girls. I'm hungry, and that strawberry shortcake sure looks delicious!" On the way back, the lady placed the flowers carefully around her wrist.

MEET CHLOE!
by Tim Rehm

Chloe is a long-haired Chihuahua
who was born on December 1, 2005.
When she gets excited, don't be surprised
if you hear her talk to you!
She has been known to say "Love you!"
Always friendly and playful, Chloe loves cuddling
in bed under the blankets.
She also enjoys running around outside with
the Flowerpot Bunnies.
And, of course, she definitely enjoys the
occasional treat. Her favorite is a nice
scoop of peanut butter!
This cute, inquisitive Chihuahua has been
a wonderful pet, and her unique personality
has brought joy to our family.

Flowers By Emily

    Flowers add color and beauty to the world around us. They are important in creating new plants. Small animals and insects are attracted to the flower and carry its pollen to another flower. We use flowers to brighten our homes and bring cheer to others.

    Each type of flower has a different meaning that has been passed down from one generation to the next. Here are some of my favorite flowers and what they symbolize.

Peony
happy life

Daisy
innocence and loyal love

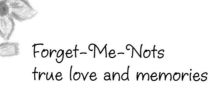

Forget-Me-Nots
true love and memories

Johnny Jump-Ups
thinking of you

Hydrangea
thank you for understanding

Tulip
perfect love and grace

Sunflower
loyalty, warmth, and adoration

Astilbe
friendship

Rosetta's Woods

The Hosta Patch

"Rosetta"

Sparkling Waters

Evergreen Woods

The Tiny House

Begonia Island